TALKING IT THROUGH

Rosie's First Day at School

Rosemary Stones

Illustrated by Christopher O'Neill

Happy Cat Books

On her first day at school Rosie feels shy.
Gemma gives her hand a lick when Rosie says goodbye.
Mum and baby Thomas wave.

Rosie's teacher is Ms Howard.
She is nice with a friendly face.
She shows the children where to hang up their things.
Rosie has a clown picture over her peg.

But while Rosie is at school, what are mum and baby
Thomas and Gemma doing?

They are at the market.
"We'll have a special tea today, Thomas," says mum,
"for Rosie's first day at big school. What shall we have?"
"Banas," says Thomas. Thomas likes bananas.
"Sweety," he says.
Gemma wags her tail. Gemma likes sweets.

But while mum and Thomas and Gemma are shopping,
what is Rosie doing?

Ms Howard tells her children they are in Blue class.
Rosie sits at a table with Tara and Zoe and Bhupinder.
Rosie wonders if she will ever remember the names of all
the children in her class. There are so many!
Ms Howard is very good at remembering.
"Here you are Rosie," she says as she gives her a nice big
sheet of paper for drawing. "And there's one for you,
Bhupinder!"

But while Rosie is doing her drawing, what is Gemma
doing?

Gemma is worried.

Where is Rosie?

Gemma paws at the door. She wants to go and find her.
"Rosie hasn't forgotten you, Gemma! She will play with
you after school," says mum.

But while Gemma is waiting by the door for her, what is
Rosie doing?

It is playtime.
Rosie and her new friends are watching all the big children rushing round.
At first they feel nervous but then Zoe suggests they play Chase.
Soon they are running round too.

But while Rosie is trying to catch
Bhupinder, what are mum and baby
Thomas doing?

Baby Thomas is trying to walk.
Quite often he sits down with a bang on his bottom.
But he always wants to try again.
"Well done, Thomas!" says mum. "Soon you'll be able to walk
Rosie to school."

But while mum is helping baby Thomas, what is Rosie doing?

Rosie wants to go to the toilet and so does Tara. They whisper in Ms Howard's ear. "Even the Queen goes to the toilet," says Ms Howard, "so it's all right to ask! Who else wants to go?" Lots of children put up their hand and Ms Howard takes them.

But while Rosie and Tara are washing their hands, what are mum and baby Thomas doing?

They are having lunch.

Thomas likes his scrambled egg.

So does Gemma.

"Rosie will be having her first school dinner," says mum.

"I hope she likes it …"

Is Rosie going to have a nice dinner?

Rosie is having chicken with mashed potato in a ball.
For pudding she has chosen custard with upside down cake.
Zoe is vegetarian and she is having baked bean lasagne.

It is very noisy in the dining room.
"Quieten down, children!" says Mrs Johns. She is the headteacher.
After dinner the children go out to play again.

But while Rosie is in the playground, what are baby Thomas and
Gemma doing?

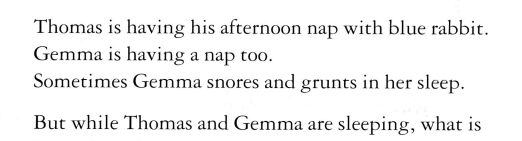

Thomas is having his afternoon nap with blue rabbit.
Gemma is having a nap too.
Sometimes Gemma snores and grunts in her sleep.

But while Thomas and Gemma are sleeping, what is
Rosie doing?

It is storytime and Ms Howard is reading to her class.
She turns the book round so everyone can see the pictures.
Rosie thinks it is a good story.
It makes everyone laugh.

But while Rosie is listening to the story, what is mum doing?

Mum is putting Thomas in his buggy.
It is time to go and fetch Rosie.
Thomas is pleased. "Osie, Osie," he says.
Gemma is excited.
She won't stand still while mum puts her lead on.

But as mum and Thomas and Gemma set off to school,
what is Rosie doing?

Rosie is coming out to meet them!
She shows them her picture.
Mum thinks it is very good.
Rosie says she likes school but she is glad it is time
to go home.
Mum and baby Thomas and Gemma are glad too.

And what does Rosie do at home?

Rosie is having a special first day at school tea.
There are sausages and tomato ketchup.
There is a bowl of sweets.
And, of course, some bananas.

Tomorrow Rosie will go to school again.